First American Edition 2005
by Kane/Miller Book Publishers, Inc.
La Jolla, California

Original edition ©La Galera, SA Editorial and Círculo de Lectores, Sociedad Anónima Unipersonal,
Barcelona, Spain 2003
World rights reserved.
Original Catalan title: *Els patins d'en Sebastià*
©Joan de Déu Prats, 2003 for the text
©Francesc Rovira, 2003 for the illustrations

All rights reserved. For more information contact:
Kane/Miller Book Publishers, Inc.
P.O. Box 8515
La Jolla, CA 92038
www.kanemiller.com

Library of Congress Control Number: 2005923347

Printed and Bound in China by Regent Publishing Services Ltd.

2 3 4 5 6 7 8 9 10

ISBN 1-929132-81-6

Sebastian's Roller Skates

Written by Joan de Déu Prats   Illustrated by Francesc Rovira

Kane/Miller
BOOK PUBLISHERS

Sebastian didn't talk very much, even though he had a lot to say.
Sebastian was shy. He was very shy.

The neighbors would say, "My goodness Sebastian, you're getting tall!"

And Sebastian would look at the floor, nod his head, and blush.
What he wanted to say though, was that someday he'd like to be tall enough
to reach every single button in the elevator, even the ones at the very top.

But Sebastian didn't talk very much.

"How's school?" the barber would ask, wrapping Sebastian in a cape.

And Sebastian would look down at his feet, blush, and whisper, "Fine." What he wanted to say though, was that he loved geography, and that he knew the names of faraway seas, tropical islands and distant lands.

When the barber was finished he'd ask Sebastian how he liked his haircut. And in a very small voice, Sebastian would whisper, "Fine," again. What he wanted to say though, was that if the barber made his head look like a billiard ball next time, he'd regret it.

4

Sebastian didn't talk very much. Not in the elevator. Not in the barbershop. Not in school.

When the teacher would ask him to name the capital of Iceland, or the capital of Mongolia, or the capital of Burundi, Sebastian would just look down at his desk, because even though he knew the answers, he couldn't seem to say anything.

Sebastian sat in the last row, right behind Ester. Ester had curly hair and eyes the color of honey. Sebastian liked Ester, but he'd never spoken to her.

After school, Sebastian always walked home through the park. One afternoon, he noticed a pair of old roller skates. Sebastian had never skated before, but he'd always wanted to try. He waited a few minutes, and when no one appeared, he decided to try them on.

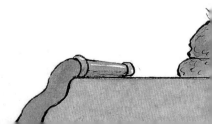

He stood up very slowly, took a careful step and…
Whammmm! Right on his rear end!

He tried again. And again, the same thing happened.

"Skating is not for me," Sebastian thought. He took off the skates,
put them back on the bench, and walked home.

The next day, when Sebastian walked through the park, he saw that the skates were still there, right where he had left them.

Sebastian scratched his nose. He looked right. He looked left. Nobody was around.

This time he was able to stand up, and stay up.
But when he tried to take a step, he fell.

At least he'd stood up!

Maybe he should take the skates home...

After that, Sebastian went to the park every day after school to practice.

He always went slowly and carefully, taking tiny steps until he could grab on to something - a lamp post, a tree, a railing. Once, he even tried to grab on to someone's moustache!

Sebastian skated every day, and every day he got a little bit better, but after a week he still couldn't go very far or very fast. Then he saw some other skaters gliding by, as if it were the easiest thing in the world. He sat down on the bench, sad and a tiny bit heartbroken. Then he went home.

He was back the next afternoon though. He put the skates on, and then, just like always, he started to skate very slowly, first one foot, then the other.

He was concentrating so hard, he didn't hear the shouting,
"My dog! Somebody, please! Help me catch my dog!"

Suddenly, a big dog was licking his face. Sebastian had to grab him to keep from falling down.

Just then, the dog started to run, and somehow, Sebastian managed to hold on to the leash. What happened next is something Sebastian could never have imagined - he skated as if he were a water skier, gliding gracefully behind the big dog.

They crossed the bridge over the pond, they crossed the path that led to the grove, they crossed the playground with the swings – they even jumped over a ditch where workers were repairing a pipe. Sebastian kept his balance the whole time, until finally, the dog stopped running.

The dog's owner came for her dog, but Sebastian just stood there. He'd skated through practically the whole park! He could hardly believe it!

When he got back to his apartment building, a neighbor was waiting for the elevator.

"How are things, Sebastian?" the neighbor asked.

At first Sebastian didn't say anything. He started to shrug like he usually did, but then he stopped. His face brightened, and he answered without thinking, "Great! I'm learning how to roller skate."

24

The next day was Saturday, and Sebastian spent the whole morning skating without ever worrying about falling down. He skated through the whole park, and even though he did fall down twice, both times he got up right away and kept on skating.

Sebastian began to worry less about other things, too.

When he had to go to the barbershop again, and the barber asked, "How's school?" Sebastian did not lower his eyes or answer in a whisper. Instead, he just opened his mouth…"I know the names of all the most important deserts in the world and where they are: the Sahara in Africa, the Gobi in Asia, and the Atacama in South America."

"How about that?" smiled the barber in surprise.

"And this time I don't want my head to look like a billiard ball!"

When Sebastian left the barbershop, he could hardly believe what he had done. He had a lot to say, and he'd said it!

So now, when the teacher asked, "Let's see, who knows the names of the tallest mountains in the world?" Sebastian would put up his hand and answer, "Mount Everest, Qogir, and Kangchenjunga."

He still had something else he wanted to do though. So one afternoon, when he saw Ester, the little girl with curly hair, he made up his mind.

He didn't fall very much anymore when he skated, and sometimes when he had a lot to say, he said it, so he walked over to Ester and asked with a smile, "Would you like to go skating with me?" And guess what? Ester was a little bit shy. But she did whisper, "Yes."

Sebastian went home feeling very happy. He broke his piggy bank and ran to the store to buy himself a new pair of skates. Then he went to the park and returned the old roller skates to the same bench where he had found them.

He thought maybe somebody else who didn't talk very much even when they had a lot to say might also like to learn how to skate.